moshi monsters™

pick Your Path

Moshling Mayhem

2

Published by Ladybird Books Ltd 2011
A Penguin Company
Penguin Books Ltd, 80 Strand, London, WC2R 0RL, UK
Penguin Group (USA) Inc., 375 Hudson Street, New York 10014, USA
Penguin Books Australia Ltd, Camberwell Road, Camberwell, Victoria 3124,
Australia (A division of Pearson Australia Group Pty Ltd)
Penguin Group (NZ), 67 Apollo Drive, Rosedale, Auckland 0632,
New Zealand (a division of Pearson New Zealand Ltd)
Canada, India, South Africa

Sunbird is a trade mark of Ladybird Books Ltd

© Mind Candy Ltd. Moshi Monsters is a trademark
of Mind Candy Ltd. All rights reserved.

By Ian Pike

www.ladybird.com

ISBN: 978-1-40939 - 0817
011
Printed in Great Britain

www.greenpenguin.co.uk

To claim your exclusive virtual gift,
go to the sign-in page of
MOSHIMONSTERS.COM
And enter the fourth word on the twentieth
line of the fifteenth page of this book!
Your surprise free gift will appear
in your treasure chest!

'Weeeeeee!' shouts ShiShi the Sneezing Panda as she swings from the curtains. **Spppllllaaattt!!** goes a large, gooey piece of Roarberry Cheesecake straight into the face of Fumble the Acrobatic Seastar. You look around in shock and can hardly believe your eyes. It was thrown by Gigi the Magical Mule. Of all the Moshlings!

'What the, who, why and . . . what?' you mumble to yourself in confusion.

You stare around Buster's ranch in horror; never having seen so much mess and chaos. The Moshlings have lost it completely and are behaving really, really badly. Something terrible must have happened to them to make them go off the rails like this. Right now you just don't have time to work out what that might be though. You are under attack as the naughty Moshlings have you in their sights!

Glllappppp!!!

You duck down on the floor to avoid some flying Beanie Blobs that a bunch of Worldies are currently using as ammunition. Something is very wrong here. And you don't just mean the plant pot that's being used as a football and currently heading towards you at great speed. There can be no other explanation for it. The Moshlings have turned rotten. You look round desperately for Buster in the hope that he can explain. However, there's no sign of him. Taking care to avoid a couple of Kitties, who are busy spreading Quenut Butter on the sofa, you rush around madly, ducking to avoid being a target.

'Buster!' you shout, dodging a bunch of mid-air Sludge Fudge travelling in your general direction. 'Where are you?'

'Back here,' Buster shouts out from a corner. 'They've pinned me in. I'll create a diversion so you can reach me.'

Buster runs out and takes a shot of fudge to the face, but he's definitely working as a distraction.

'That the best you got? Come on! Give it another shot!' he shouts as another big splodge of Sludge Fudge catches him full on the nose. Still, it gives you time to make a run to his newly formed den.

Dodge. Weave. Whoops!

It's not the easiest journey. A load of Moshlings have got you marked out for splatting but you just about make it across the room. You scuttle behind the Gumball Machine and an out of breath Buster joins you.

'Little rats. It's taken me half an hour already to get all the molten goo out of my hat, and don't even get me started on what they did to my bed.'

Wow! He really is in a state. All you can see (apart from a pair of eyes) are his hat and whiskers and they are both covered in gloop. He's dressed from head to toe in the stuff.

'What's going on Buster?' you yell over the noise. 'One of the Moshlings just tried to bite my ankle as I somersaulted over the sofa to escape from Jeepers the Snuggly Tiger Cub. He tried to throw a can of Swoonafish at me!'

Buster looks at you, wiping a handful of gloop out of one eye so he can peer back properly.

'They've been like that all day. Just suddenly turned . . . out of the blue. Good as gold one second . . . then naughty as can be the next. Honestly, at one point it was so bad I had to barricade myself in the cupboard. I've never known anything like it from a Moshling . . . and I've been chasing them since I was knee-high to Mr Snoodle!'

You pop your head round the Gumball Machine to see if the situation out there has improved at all, then just as quickly pop it right back in again. Jeepers has an evil glint in his eye and a can of Swoonafish raised and ready. He manages to hurl one, but you get out of the way just in time. This really is serious stuff.

Do you take on Jeepers? If so, **turn to page 55.**

Or do you stay and carry on the battle with Buster? In which case, **turn to page 13.**

7

You screech into The Port. Strangeglove is nowhere to be seen. At least the Moshlings here seem to be behaving. It would be hard enough to deal with Strangeglove's evil ways and try to control a load of extra naughtiness.

Suddenly, out of nowhere, a Glump flies past your head and lands with a thud near the water's edge. It looks at you sadly, dribbling out of one corner of its mouth.

'I see you've met Freakface, the latest addition to the clan,' Strangeglove calls out as he appears from the shadows, smirking at you.

'Mw-ha-ha-ha.' He laughs evilly, then stops just as quickly as he started. 'Sorry about that. Just thinking about a very funny joke I heard yesterday.'

He is standing next to an evil-looking contraption. Suddenly a couple of passing Moshlings are sucked into it and, just as fast, are fired out the other end as Glumps.

'Welcome to my world, Bruiser and Fishlips. Mw-ha-ha-ha. That joke really was terribly good. You see . . .'

You cut him off short.

'Never mind that. Stop glumping those Moshlings.'

Another three are dragged in by an invisible force, then fired out as Glumps. If this carries on much longer there won't be a normal Moshling left in Monstro City.

'Never! It's all part of the master plan. Phase one: Sweet Tooth and I find more and more evil uses for the sweets. Phase two: meet my most cunning Glump-a-tron yet. Faster and more ferocious than anything before.'

Saying that, he turns up the dial and three more

Moshlings are wickedly glumped.

You move towards Strangeglove, knowing he won't give in without a fight. You were right.

'Look at that one. What a very funny moustache,' he chuckles evilly.

'Stop it at once Strangeglove . . . or . . .'

'Or what? You think you scare me?' he smirks.

A couple of passing Katsumas see what you are up against and try to help.

You stand in front of Strangeglove, your new menacing furry allies behind you.

'You think they worry me? Ha!' Strangeglove is doing his best to hide the fact that he is clearly a bit rattled by you all ganging up on him.

'My work here is done anyway.' He hits a button and the Glump-a-tron starts dragging in Moshlings at twice the speed. If you don't do something soon, the prospect is just too hideous to think about.

'Mw-ha-ha . . . what a joke it was. Hilarious.' He cackles as he turns and runs off down Ooh La Lane, Sweet Tooth scuttling along at his side.

The Katsumas give chase immediately in an attempt to stop Strangeglove from escaping.

If you think it best to stay and deal with the Glump-a-tron, **turn to page 64.**

If you want to help the Katsumas go after Strangeglove, **turn to page 36.**

As you try to come up with a plan to cope with the Birdies, matters come to a head and force you to snap into action. Tiki the Pilfering Toucan manages to snaffle your watch. Prof. Purplex the Owl of Wiseness uses every ounce of his wisdom to pluck a large heavy book from the shelf and hurl it directly at your head.

You can feel yourself beginning to get cross.

'Right, that does it. I want my watch back and . . .'

DJ Quack, Peppy and the Prof. are giggling to themselves in the corner.

'Suppose you think this is clever?'

'Mee, mee mee mee mee mee mee mee.' You can hardly believe it. Peppy is actually mimicking you.

'I want my watch back!'

Tiki snorts back a laugh and shuffles about shiftily. Honestly you have never seen such bad behaviour.

'I don't want to have to say it again, thank you. And don't think I don't know what you're up to, Prof.'

Out of the corner of your eye you spot him lugging a big encyclopedia onto a rocking chair, then pulling it back as far as it will rock. He's going to launch it at you, using the chair as some sort of throwing device.

'Missile attack. Duck for cover,' you shout, flinging yourself on the floor. The book hurtles past you, narrowly missing your head. Phew! You turn back to Tiki.

'My watch please. Now.'

Tiki sighs then reaches behind him and hands over a banana instead. This is too much for the others and they dissolve into fits of laughter. However you have had enough.

'Right! That's it. This has got to stop. I'm extremely disappointed in all of you.'

More sniggering and shuffling about but at least you have their attention for a brief moment.

'This is not the behaviour expected of a Moshling.' You are letting them have it with both barrels but just then the Prof. lets you have something of his own making.

'Buuurrrppp!'

You can hardly believe it of the Prof. as the others dissolve in fits of sniggering. And right in your face too.

'It's not just yourselves you're letting down here you know.'

You wait for a second to see if any of this is sinking in. Well, they've stopped snorting tears of laughter for a minute. Something must be working. Tiki even shamefacedly holds out your watch.

'Thank you. Now the rest of you could learn a lot from that. So do we have an understanding? Whatever has been making you like this has got to end. Now!'

You look at the Birdies and your heart melts. They all look so guilty. Oh well, at least your message must be getting through. Suddenly a noise stops you short.

Bang, clash, dink, bang, dong, ding! The Birdies are drumming on the furniture with big wooden spoons and shoes and anything they can get hold of. And now DJ Quack's busy pouring a large bottle of Buster's favourite

Emergen-T down his beak.

'Glug, glug, glug!'

He's already filled up with several beakfuls. He must be planning one monster burp to rival the Prof's. But surprise, surprise he suddenly hands the bottle over meekly, then wanders slowly off for a sleep in the corner. You shake your head from side to side to see if you are dreaming. **Ow!** (Note to self. Next time you do that, move away from the wall.)

'I wonder . . .' you mutter, as the Moshlings continue to drum loudly; adding to your already spreading headache.

'Anybody fancy a little drink? Thirsty work this being naughty isn't it?' you ask.

You hold out the bottle. Keeping one eye on DJ Quack, just to make sure it's not all part of a plan to trick you. Luckily though, he's snoring away like a Hickopotamus. Tiki snatches the bottle off you.

'Manners!'

He pours most of it over the Prof. and Peppy's head before glugging a load himself. The effect is almost instant. As you make sure that the Prof. and Peppy have also taken a mouthful or two on-board, Tiki is soon calm and quiet. The Prof. wanders off to read on the rocking chair as Peppy curls up into a little ball. You realise whatever is in the sweets; the cure can be found by glugging back a drop or two of Emergen-T.

You smile quietly to yourself then wander off with the bottle to deal with the rest of the Moshlings, knowing you have saved the day!

The End

You and Buster are still very much under attack.

'What's happened to them?' you shout. 'Did they eat too much chocolate? You know what they get like after lots of sugar.' You've started whimpering nervously, desperately searching for an explanation. Buster snorts at your suggestion.

'Sugar! I mean sure, a Moshling can get a little carried away and over excited after a few gummy cubes. And I suppose they were chomping on a bag of sweets before it all happened, but this . . . ha! This, my friend is a lot more worrying than a simple case of too much sugar.'

You wrack your brains.

'Well they don't just turn from cute, fluffy little Moshlings into furry thugs overnight.'

Buster looks at you, an idea clearly forming in his brain. 'Unless someone got to them somehow?'

You don't like the way this is going. Buster can't mean . . . he does. The name that can strike fear into the heart of any Moshi Monster.

'Not . . . Dr. Strangeglove?'

'Well look out there. They've well and truly flipped.'

You stick your head back out of hiding for a brief second to check. Luckily for you, most of the Moshlings seem to have got bored of hounding you. They're now pulling all the feathers out of the cushions and flinging them at Purdy the Tubby Huggishi. That would normally make poor Purdy terribly upset. However, she now only seems interested in fighting back.

Your eyes take in the sorry scene before you. Moshlings running amok. Moshlings jumping on each other. Moshlings breaking things.

'So you think Dr. Strangeglove has turned them bad?' you ask Buster in shock.

'Well how else do you explain it? Mark my words; this has got his handiwork written all over it.'

'What makes you so sure?' you ask.

'Actually, he left a note, look.'

I turned them all rotten.

Mwa, ha, ha.

Yours sincerely,

Dr. Strangelove.

'If it isn't down to him . . . I'll eat my hat,' Buster says.

You look at Buster's hat and doubt it. Not with that amount of Gloop currently on the brim. However, he does make a fair point.

'But how on earth did he manage it? There are just so many Moshlings,' you say.

Buster wipes a big gloopy sludge dribble off the end of his nose and sniffs deeply to clear the rest.

'My guess would be those sweets had a secret ingredient in them to make Moshlings turn naughty.'

You scratch your head. Naughty sweets! Well, it wouldn't be the first time sweets have been tampered with in Monstro City! Buster leans over to you and whispers, 'I smell something rotten. And I'm not just talking about the fact that the Foodies seem to have given up washing. Strangeglove must have put together another super-fiendish, evil concoction. A sweet created with the express intention of causing as much mayhem as possible. Something so extraordinarily wicked as to turn all the Moshlings really, really, very bad indeed.'

You stare at him in horror.

'You don't mean . . .'

Daaan, daan, daan!

A couple of the Moshlings have jumped on the piano and are thumping up and down on the keys with their furry feet all covered in Quenut Butter. However, you can't worry about that right now. There are far more serious matters to attend to.

'But that's terrible.'

'I'll bet you a dime to a dollar he's still handing them out. Or at least that rotten accomplice of his, Sweet Tooth, will be. And if they are, pretty soon we could lose every Moshling to naughtiness.' Buster looks very worried.

As you wonder what to do, you become aware that things in the ranch are taking a turn for the worse.

You can either stay here and try to help Buster bring these Moshlings under control. **Turn to page 53.**

Or head into Monstro City and go after the dastardly Dr. Strangeglove. **Turn to page 43.**

You are frantically continuing your search for the other missing Fluffies when you hear a little whimper. You look round. There it is again. The sound of a Moshling in distress and it's coming from behind that rockery. You creep round slowly and find Dipsy the Dinky Dreamcloud, sobbing away all by herself. You slink across nervously. If your experiences of today have taught you anything, it's never trust a Moshling while they're under the influence of a magic sweet. But Dipsy does look very upset so you keep moving ever closer.

'Are you OK?' you ask gently.

You just about hear Dipsy's whimpering response.

'So you're not OK,' you say.

Dipsy actually seems a little scared. There's even a little tear running down her cloudy face. You edge closer.

'What's the matter?' you ask.

From the sniffing you manage to work out that Dipsy is actually worried by suddenly finding herself being naughty. She is really very concerned about the way her and the rest of the Fluffies have trashed the Moshling Gardens.

'Don't worry. It'll be all right. But I really need to find the others, or they'll just carry on being very badly behaved. We don't want that now, do we?'

The answer turns out to be both yes and no as you quickly discover. Dipsy may not like the effect the sweets have had on her but that doesn't stop her from being naughty.

'Ow. Will you stop that?' you cry as you begin the search for the other Fluffies, trying to fend off a Dipsy attack at the same time. 'Where exactly are they?'

Dipsy manages to behave just long enough for you to discover that the others are lurking behind the fountain, so you make your way quietly over towards them.

You can hear sniggering, scuffling about and in one or two cases what sounds for all the world like burping. Normally, a Moshling as delicate as Dipsy wouldn't find it in the slightest bit amusing. But with her new naughty personality, she seems to think it is the funniest thing she's ever heard. Oh well, at least she has stopped crying.

'Ssshhh! Please Dipsy. If they hear us we'll never catch them.'

You look round to see if there's anything you could use to snare them in. Once you've managed to sneak up behind them, and if Dipsy can stop laughing, you might be able to catch them by surprise.

You spot an old basket that the Roarkers must have been using to carry plants in. You creep forwards. As you close in on the fountain you hear more giggling, shuffling and yes, unfortunately, a lot more burping. You edge ever nearer . . .

Within a matter of seconds you are just a short reach away from snaring your targets. You raise the basket high above your head and shuffle forward silently. Like a Katsuma on the prowl you sneak closer and closer. And then, just as you are about to pounce, Dipsy dissolves in another fit of laughter.

The other Moshlings turn in surprise. The second they see you, they're ready to dash off. Luckily you are far too quick for them and pounce like a flash.

'Gotcha, Fluffies!'

In the blink of an eye the basket is shut and the Moshlings are inside. They carry on burping away merrily but at least they're contained. There's now just the small matter of Dipsy to deal with. Luckily for you, she's still laughing so hard she definitely won't be in any position to behave badly for a while. Well done! Not only have you trapped the escaping Fluffies but you've also managed to cheer up and look after one very scared Dreamcloud.

The End

Having decided to head to The Puzzle Palace, you have to make a quick detour. Bushy needs to round up her trusty pack of Musky Husky Puppies to help the search. Luckily they are on a strict diet from Bushy to keep them trim for tracking, so they haven't eaten any of the dodgy sweets.

'D'you really think we'll find them, Bushy?' you ask, worried they may be too far away and too well hidden.

'Trust me,' she says, leashing together a couple of eager and excitable Musky Huskies. 'If I can hunt out an Abominable Furi in a howling snow blizzard then a couple of Moshlings will be a piece of Roarberry Cheesecake.'

Now ready for action you spur onwards to The Puzzle Palace. You are deep in thought when it hits you.

'Ow!' you shout.

A naughty Fishie has just hurled a water bomb at you and then swum off laughing. As you stand there shaking your sore head and wondering when all the mischief will end, another water bomb hits Bushy.

'Right. I'm not staying out here. It's time for us to round up those Fluffies.' With a flash of fur she disappears into the Palace. You are not sure whether to follow her. As you stand in thought, another water bomb hits you.

To follow Bushy into the Palace and help round up the lost Fluffies, **turn to page 45.**

Or if you think you should stay here and deal with the water bomb attack, **turn to page 74.**

You arrive in the Dress Up room to find the Spookies are not going to let themselves be captured easily. For starters they've made such a mess in there it's impossible to get through the door, never mind capture them. One minute you feel you might be just millimetres away from grabbing one, but just as you get close it disappears under a Madame Macabre Cloak.

'Stop that will you? Where have you gone?' you shout desperately. Reaching out for what you thought was a cunningly disguised Spookie, you discover it's just a large Frilly White Dress swinging on a rail.

'Come on guys. I know you are in there,' you call out as a Patterned Blue Shawl rushes past with a Moshling hidden inside. They're having the best time ever but you're getting very flustered. Chasing them round in circles, reaching out to grab hold, only to then find you have nothing but a Blue Feather Boa in your hand.

And then it occurs to you. Your mission here was to track at least some of the naughty Moshlings down and stop them wreaking havoc out in Monstro City. Well, these ones at least are all nicely contained and nothing is actually getting damaged. Your work is kind of done. And now you think about it, this really could be a lot of fun.

'Right, that's it. I'm coming in.'

You leap into the pile of dress up clothes on the floor. This game is a great laugh and should keep everyone occupied until the effects of the sweets wear off.

The End

You arrive in the Fun Park puffing and panting and totally out of breath. Things are a little calmer down here with just a few Moshlings causing trouble. They are taking more than their fair share of turns on the rides, jumping the queue and shoving each other around. Some of them are still acting normally. But for how long? And then you spy them. Strangeglove and Sweet Tooth are off in the distance, leaving bags of sweets where innocent Moshlings might find them and fall under their evil spell. You set off, hot on the trail.

'Stop right there. I know exactly what you're up to,' you call out breathlessly.

Strangeglove turns, surprised. 'And what might that be?' he replies.

'Turning the Moshlings bad. I know about the sweets.'

Just to prove your point, a few of the previously well behaved Moshlings suddenly start fighting with each other. This really is getting out of hand.

'Clever, for one so young,' Sweet Tooth says, toying with the hypno-blaster lollipop.

'To be fair Buster worked it out, but now I'm here to put a stop to it.'

'Buster Bumblechops! Such a shame he couldn't be here himself to witness this. Mw-ha-ha-ha-ha,' Strangeglove laughs.

You look at him in horror. He simply pats himself on the back in response.

'Sorry about that. Just clearing my throat.'

'How could you have invented a formula so hideous?'

'It's taken years of planning. Luckily young Sweet Tooth here had already stumbled across something that worked. I saw the effects and realised I could use them to my own evil ends. Then all I had to do was double the dosage and watch the fabulous outcome on these horrid little Moshlings.'

You decide enough is enough.

'Hand over the sweets, Strangeglove, and you Sweet Tooth. You don't scare me.' (They do if the truth be told, but you cannot let them see that.)

Strangeglove looks at you. You stare back. You step forward menacingly. He steps backwards. You both realise you look like you are dancing so stand still. Finally he turns on his heel and runs away, laughing as he goes.

'You really think you can stop me? My next invention will make these sweets seem like child's play. Mw-ha-ha-ha. Sorry do you have a lozenge? This throat of mine really is very tickly.'

And with that he heads to The Port to wreak even more havoc.

To follow Dr. Strangeglove down to The Port and put a stop to his evil plan, **turn to page 8.**

Moments later, the hungry Dinos are perched on a wall wearing what can only be described as a blanket of Sludge Fudge. At least you think they are. You can barely see because there is a lot of icky, sticky stuff currently running down your own face too. When they said they were hungry, what they really meant was they were hoping to have a couple of mouthfuls then wash each other's fur with it, before doing the same to you. You sigh deeply, spit out a globule and try to work out what to do next.

'Come on guys. If you keep this up for too long I'll have no fur left,' you cry out as Doris starts conditioning your head with a bucketful of Slug Slurp Slushie.

'And thank you, but I really don't think I need it all combed out with a garden rake. It's actually quite sore,' you tell Gurgle.

You try and wipe off a combination of Sludge Fudge and Slug Slurp Slushie shampoo. Not easy when your hairdressers are currently trying their best to wedge a bucket on your head.

As you sort yourself out they look a little hurt. Gurgle is actually having an almighty tantrum, stamping his feet in a fit of anger. Doris is sitting with her back to you in one major sulk.

'Come on everyone, don't be like that. I still think my fur looks lovely, only I really need to be getting on.'

Out of the corner of your eye you've spotted Pooky and Snookums in the barn. They seem to have discovered a great game that involves chucking all the straw around.

So much so that the air is now totally filled with straw and it's actually quite hard to see where they are. Now might be a good time to step in, so you move towards the barn, trying to ignore the ferociously loud cries and whimpers from Doris and Gurgle.

'I'm just going to deal with the . . . No I really do like it, it's just . . . please don't look at me like that, Gurgle.'

You splutter your way over to the barn. This is really hard. Everything you try and do just makes things worse and worse. There doesn't actually seem to be any way to get the Moshlings back on track.

'Whoa!'

You've just walked into a straw storm. It's blinding and making you sneeze, splutter and cough. You hold your paw up in front of your face but can barely make it out.

'Where are you?' you shout, trying your hardest not to inhale a bale of straw.

And then, out of nowhere, they strike. An ambush of the worst possible kind. Terrifying and like nothing you could ever imagine. A tickle attack. You are cornered and there is no escape.

'Hhhheeellppp!' you cry out in vain and to no avail.

And then just as suddenly as it started, it stops. It all goes quiet. You breathe a huge sigh of relief as the straw begins to settle. They must have moved on. But sadly no. Shadows appear in the air. Snookums swinging from the rafters. Pooky arming herself, then stuffing straw down your neck. And Gurgle and Doris have stopped sulking enough to enlist in their army. As the straw fight kicks off once again, this time even worse than before, you curse Dr. Strangeglove and his evil sweets. Perhaps there's only one thing to be done.

'If you can't beat 'em, join 'em,' you shout. You grab a handful of straw and hurl it with all your might at Snookums.

'Take that,' you yell, as you begin the ultimate straw attack.

The End

'This is the right thing to do. Definitely,' you tell yourself.

You rush about trying to find enough food to tempt Raarghly into telling you exactly where Dewy is. You know that once you've found him, you still have to persuade him to help you find a way to shut down the Glump-a-tron. And even then there's no guarantee he'll be able to do it.

'Here!' you shout, shovelling a plateful of Zoot Fruit forward.

'Mmmmnnngggghhh,' chews Raarghly devouring it in seconds. 'Still hungry.'

'Try this,' you push forward a massive bowlful of Gloop Soup.

'Nice.' Down it goes in one. 'But not enough,' says Raarghly.

'What about this then? Now I know it's your favourite.' You hold out a yummy, scrummy Eyescream Sundae.

Raarghly's eyes light up. 'Mmmmmnn,' he says, reaching forward greedily.

'Oh no,' you say withdrawing the carton from his reach. 'First things first. We had a deal.'

You can see Raarghly's started dribbling. He desperately wants to get his hands on that Sundae but you need one vital piece of information first.

'Tell me where I can find Dewy.'

Raarghly hesitates then reaches forward.

'Gabby's.'

You hold the carton out and Raarghly devours it in one. Then you rush off to track Dewy down.

He is sipping on a Slug Slurp Slushie and reading the latest issue of *Hammer Times* in Gabby's when you reach him.

'Dewy,' you gasp; out of breath, having run so fast. 'I need your help.'

He looks up from his magazine and takes another quick slurp of Slushie.

'If it's anything to do with what's going on with those Moshlings, then forget it. I've tried everything and they just won't listen.' He nods in the direction of a group of them trashing the counter and stealing food.

You are torn.

If you think you should ignore the Moshlings wrecking the counter and continue trying to persuade Dewy to help you, **turn to page 31.**

But if you think it best to step in and deal with the Moshlings on the rampage first, **turn to page 34.**

'OK. Here's the deal. If you'll all just try and find a way to play nicely together then maybe . . . just maybe . . . I'll get everyone a big glass of Bug Juice afterwards.'

Well that didn't work. Sooki-Yaki is attacking her own shadow while Chop Chop is busy trying to steal your shoes. Wow, this is so tough.

'What about another game then, if you don't fancy hide-and-seek? Anything you like. Just name it.'

The assorted Moshlings look at you.

'Catch? Hopscotch?'

Chop Chop yawns and nudges Sooki-Yaki who giggles. This is embarrassing. They actually think you're boring!

'All right then. Something a bit more exciting then? Who's for a bit of duck, duck, goose?'

'Eeerrrgggghhhhh.' They all groan but you decide to try it out anyway. You really have got to keep them occupied and hope the madness wears off.

'Right. This is how it works. We all sit in a circle facing each other. Then one of us walks round tapping heads saying whether they are a "duck" or a "goose". We could even make it a bit more interesting. Say call it Foodies, Foodies, Puppies . . .'

They all become very agitated at that suggestion. Each is desperate to be the centre of the game.

'Well we can't exactly play Moshlings, Moshlings, Moshlings now can we? It won't make any sense.'

But that's exactly what they want. They are currently sitting in a circle (occasionally) running round and round each other and tapping each other's heads (quite hard).

28

You hate to admit it but it does look quite good fun.

'Well, I suppose we could try playing it your way for a bit,' you say. At least they're not breaking anything or making too much mess. They stop running and look at you.

'But you're just making up the rules as you go along. It doesn't make any sense.'

However, that's just the point. That's why they seem to love it so much. And as you are finding out a lot today, sometimes doing the opposite of what you normally get up to can be quite good fun.

Chop. Swing. Chop. Chop Chop whizzes round and 'taps' you on the head.

'Ow.' That was a lot more than a tap.

Sneak. Bam. Creep. Sooki-Yaki barges into you.

'Right, my turn,' you decide. Well if you stay still much longer, you'll be covered in bruises.

Bish! Bash!

You run round them all, giving as good as you get. They laugh, loving it. You hate to admit it but this is really good fun. Round you go once more even faster.

Bosh!

'That's it guys. We've done it. We've invented our own game. Let's call it **Bish, Bash, Bosh-a-Mosh!**'

You chase each other round and round as fast as you can, doing your best to give each other a good biff or two. You're exhausted but, luckily, so are they. Mission accomplished.

The End

You rush outside with your head in a spin. You have to track down those escaped Fluffies soon or goodness knows what kind of nonsense they could get up to.

In the Moshling Garden, your worst fears have been realised. Those Fluffies have definitely been here and boy what a mess they have made. This is serious. If those sweets of Strangeglove and Sweet Tooth's can have this kind of effect on the Fluffies, then Moshlings really could be capable of any kind of mischief.

You peer behind bushes and creep quietly around trees in the hope of catching them unawares. Occasionally you even see something white and fluffy float by. Then just as you are about to pounce, you feel a quick flick on the back of your ear and know that Honey has just pinged you. Or you catch a whiff of furniture polish and realise you must be inches away from Flumpy.

Every time, all you are left with is the sound of giggling disappearing into the distance. Or you are covered in mud from where you fell over in your haste to catch them.

But the most serious of all is a snaffle from above. An aerial attack from IGGY, clearly mistaking you for a pointy cursor. This definitely needs dealing with.

Do you continue with your search for the rest of the missing Fluffies? If so, **turn to page 16.**

Or do you try to fend off IGGY? In which case, **turn to page 63.**

You're aware time is running out. You have to get Dewy to help you.

'How do you think you might do at shutting down a Glump-a-tron?' you ask.

You really wish you'd said that last bit a little quieter. All the Moshlings are screaming, running about in a blind panic at the very mention of the word. As Dewy's Slushie goes flying, he rises to his feet quickly.

'Guess the only way to get a bit of peace is to help you then? I'll fetch my tools.'

As you rush back to the Glump-a-tron your mind is a whirl. So much to do and so little time.

You reach the Glump-a-tron and watch in terror as Moshlings everywhere hurtle towards it, only to be churned out as Glumps. Dewy stops in shock.

'Wow! That is powerful,' he exclaims.

He looks at the Glump-a-tron, doing his best to avoid a new Glump as it fires out, narrowly missing him.

'Think you can do anything with it?' you ask.

He slides himself under the main body of the machinery and looks up.

'It's not going to be easy. Pass me that spanner.'

You do so.

'Now the double threaded screwdriver . . . good. And the wrench. Excellent. And finally the hammer.'

'What do you need the hammer for?' you ask. He's been making an awful lot of mess. Parts, nuts, bolts and bits everywhere and it doesn't really seem to be making any difference. So far you really don't have a lot of faith in his efforts. Especially once he picks up the hammer and starts whacking at the Glump-a-tron from below.

'Careful!' you shout. 'That thing's dangerous.'

'It's making me feel a whole lot better,' he calls back. 'This stupid machine's impossible. I can't even get the back off.'

Thwack!

One more big thud to the metal casing and chaos ensues. The machine whirs into a fever pitch and Moshlings are still hurtling towards the Glump-a-tron from miles around. Pretty soon there won't be a single Moshling left.

'Stop it, Dewy. Look what you've done.'

But all Dewy can do now is keep on whacking away with his hammer. Unfortunately with every hit, the Glump-a-tron just becomes more and more powerful. And fatter. With every Moshling it swallows it just keeps expanding like some sort of big, chubby python. And now nothing seems to be coming out of the other end. It's completely blocked.

'She's going to blow!' you call out to Dewy. 'Get yourself out of there.'

He doesn't need telling twice and is soon beating a hasty retreat as the Glump-a-tron swells up and up. Steam starts emerging and it begins to shake and rattle.

BBBBBBAAAAAAANNNGGGGG!!!!

(That doesn't even come close to describing the noise of the Glump-a-tron exploding. But it's as close as you can get. Boy, what a sound!)

There is smoke everywhere as well as dust and fur. You spot Dewy looking round confused as Moshlings rain down like furry hailstones.

'You OK?'

He has slightly singed eyebrows and a soot-covered face but otherwise seems all right. You both check out the surroundings as the air clears. Relieved looking Moshlings are lying about confused but otherwise unharmed.

'They're fine,' you shout happily. 'The Glump-a-tron self destructed.'

'Told you all it needed was a good whack with a hammer,' says Dewy, his voice filled with relief.

Still, as long as the Moshlings are safe once again. Now all you have to do is deal with the naughty ones . . .

The End

The Moshlings really are making a mess of the cafe and it won't have a counter much longer unless you can stop them.

'Right you lot,' you call out. 'Enough's enough.'

But you know from experience they won't listen. It's time for a distraction.

'OK, everyone. Who knows any good jokes?'

They stop trashing the place for a second, turning to listen. However, you can tell from their faces that you had better be good or they'll kick off again.

'All right, I'll go first.' You desperately wrack your brains for a joke they might like.

'OK, I've got one. What do you call a magic ice scream?'

They all look at each other confused.

'Coolio the Magical Sparklepop, of course.' Not the best joke ever, but you were making it up on the spot.

'Right, here's another one then. Which ancient monument spends all day looking in the mirror?'

They are now just staring at you but that's fine, as long as they're not breaking up the shop. You just have to keep the gags coming.

'It's obvious. Cleo the Pretty Pyramid,' you say, answering your own question.

They may not be laughing but at least you have their attention. As long as you can keep on thinking of jokes you can stop them from rampaging. Dewy even gives you a wink as he grabs his tools and sneaks off while you're distracting the Moshlings. You hope he's heading down to The Port to destroy that Glump-a-tron!

But will you be able to think of enough jokes to tell the Moshlings to keep them here in the meantime? You'd better start thinking hard . . .

Moments later, you hear a huge KABOOM! in the distance. Dewy must have destroyed the Glump-a-tron!

The End

You and the Katsumas give chase, pinning Strangeglove and Sweet Tooth down in the dead end of an alleyway. Strangeglove turns to look at you. Your furry allies are ready for action. Claws out, paws moving swiftly through the air, showing him their best moves.

'You really think I'm bothered?' Strangeglove laughs.

'Well you should be . . .' you reply, chopping the air and kicking out your right leg before spinning round and giving a double wave left, ninja-style.

They do look a little concerned. 'Is that some sort of a black belt karate move?' Sweet Tooth asks.

You look away apologetically. 'No . . . actually, I have an itchy foot. This, however, is.'

Doing your best to copy the Katsumas, you leap about looking like you know what you are doing. It doesn't work. Strangeglove stands his ground, sneering at your efforts. Just then, a shadow appears overhead. The CLONC airship is above you, blocking out the light. Glump faces peer out at you and seconds later a couple of ropes are lowered down. Before you can stop them, Strangeglove and Sweet Tooth grab on and are hauled skywards to freedom.

'So long, suckers! We'd love to stay and chat, but plans to make, Moshlings to glump!' Strangeglove shouts down as the airship moves away.

'There's always next time, Strangeglove!' you call out. You hope against all hope that the effects of the sweets wear off soon and life can return to normal.

The End

As you arrive in the Underground Disco you immediately spot Tyra Fangs. She is surrounded by a crowd of monsters hanging on her every word. She is gossiping her way through the latest news in Monstro City, pausing only to check her make-up or demand a fresh drink.

'And according to Roary, the whole thing started after that horrible Sweet Tooth appeared with those sweets. That's why the Moshlings are all going completely doo-lally and apparently there's much, much worse to come if Dr. Strangeglove has his way . . .'

You manage to get a quick word in while she draws breath. She's clearly very much enjoying being the centre of attention but you have a job to do. Those escaped Fluffies are still out there on the loose.

'I understand you were the last person to see them, Tyra . . . If you could just tell me where they might be I can try to retrieve them.'

She looks you over, bats her eyelashes up and down for a second and then takes another long sip of her drink.

'I did see them. But they weren't Fluffies. Oh no, these were far, far scarier.'

Not Fluffies. But worse. What could she mean?

She smiles at her adoring gathering then leans in closer.

'What I saw were some very, very badly behaved . . . Spookies!'

You reel back in shock as you now have a major dilemma. Do you continue to try and track down the

Fluffies or go after the Spookies?

'Do you know where the Spookies are now?' you ask, your mind in a whirl.

'Not exactly. But I would guess that they were either heading for the Dress Up room or were on their way to the Market Place. It was chaos out there and hard to make out. I tell you this though, a naughty Spooky is a very troublesome creature and if someone doesn't do something soon . . .'

She lets the threat just hang there as she takes another sip of her drink and readjusts her make-up. You step away from the crowd unsure of your next move.

To seek out the Spookies in the Market Place,
go to page 65.

To look for them in the Dress Up room,
turn to page 20.

Or head back to the Moshling Garden and carry on looking for the lost Fluffies **on page 30.**

It takes some seeking out but eventually you're able to locate a Morph stone and head straight for the Candy Cane Caves. You've heard Sweet Tooth is there working on new formulas for even more lethal sweets.

You look down at the stone. What if Bushy was right? What if you glump yourself but then can't turn back? Would you be prepared to risk losing everything to protect the Moshlings? Then you catch sight of a group of Puppies behaving like you've never seen them before and realise that of course you would. If you don't, then who will?

You rub the stone and with a flash of light you can feel your body start to shake. Everything goes a little blurry. When you can see clearly again, you look down. Your heart is racing. Boy, oh boy, have you been glumped. You look a right state. And there's worse.

'Bbbuuurrrppp!!'

You can't stop burping. Great. You must have turned into some new kind of Glump called a . . .

'Bbbbbbuuurrrpppeeerrrr. A Burper. Eeewww. Gross,' you mutter to yourself.

'BURP!' Oh well, whatever it takes to get Strangeglove to trust you. You creep forward into the Candy Cane Caves. Strangeglove is there with Sweet Tooth, pouring mixtures into jars. Making his evil concoctions. A few Glumps are lolloping around in the caves so you slip in to join them, trying your best not to burp too loudly.

'That's it, Sweet Tooth. A little more of this and a lot more of that . . . this'll have those Moshlings behaving even worse than before. A-mwh-hee-hee-hee-hee-hee. What d'you think of my new evil laugh? I'm still not sure which sounds more evil the "ah" or the "ee."'

Sweet Tooth keeps on mixing so you edge nearer, aware that this might be your life forever more. A life of eternal glumpage. A fate worse than death.

'All part of my wicked master plan. Once I've finished, Monstro City will be overrun with naughty Moshlings unable to reverse the effects of the sweets. And while they are all being so badly behaved, it will be oh so easy to turn them all into Glumps. As long as they don't use the secret formula of course. That of three parts garlic marshmallows, two parts explosive bangers and mash. Mw-ha-hee-ha-hee-ha-hee. Now that definitely didn't work. I just sounded like a donkey. Let me try again.'

You have no time to lose. You're going to have to move fast. Two parts explosive bangers and mash mixed with three parts garlic marshmallows in vast quantities coming right up. As soon as all the Moshlings have swallowed that little lot they should be right as rain.

First, however, there is the small matter of being de-glumped to attend to. You burp loudly, then rub the Morph stone nervously. You wait. Nothing but another quick burp or two. Then suddenly, there is a flash of light and you are back to normal again. It worked. Now you just need to pick up the necessary supplies as quickly as possible. Then getting the antidote ready to cure all the Moshlings. It's going to be a long, long day!

The End

You head into Sludge Street, desperately searching for Dewy to help you disable the Glump-a-tron. There is no sign of him anywhere but you do spot Raarghly in the Games Starcade. He might know something. He seems to be doing quite a good job of controlling the Moshlings in there at the moment. They're shaking the machines, trying to get money out, not taking their turns, pushing in front of each other and generally arguing and fighting. However, Raarghly is moving from one to the other, just about keeping some sort of sense of order. You dash over.

'Raarghly . . . have you seen Dewy anywhere? I desperately need him to help me with something.'

Raarghly sighs wearily. 'I may have. But then again I may not. You see the thing is, dealing with all these naughty Moshlings is particularly hungry work and I've just not had time to eat,' he says, smiling knowingly.

'Please Raarghly. As soon as I find out where Dewy is, I'll get you as much space food as you can eat. This really is important.'

'And I'd love to help but I'm just too weak with hunger. It's been, oh at least an hour since I last had anything and without being fed . . .' He tails off then pounces on a couple of errant Moshlings trying to force a free game out of one of the machines.

He doesn't exactly look weak to you but you realise there's little point in arguing. Besides, the longer you spend in the Games Starcade, the more Moshlings will be turned by Sweet Tooth and Strangeglove's evil concoctions.

You have to do something and fast. But what?

Do you waste yet more precious time trying to find some suitable space food for Raarghly, in the hope he'll then lead you to Dewy? If so, **turn to page 26.**

Or do you go back to the Glump-a-tron and try to destroy it somehow on your own?
If so, **turn to page 49.**

Right. So all you need to do is track down Dr. Strangeglove. Then find some way to get him to reverse the effects of his evil sweets so all the bad Moshlings turn back into their old selves again.

You head out into Monstro City. It's chaos. Badly behaved Moshlings are everywhere causing trouble. It's up to you to deal with the situation. Not that it's going to be easy. You know Dr. Strangeglove will put up a fight if you try to stop him and you still have to find him first.

'Last I heard he was down by The Port,' Snozzle Wobbleson tells you on Main Street. He is flying about, trying to avoid the trouble.

'Word is he's invented this new hyper beam Glump-a-tron and he's turning Moshling after Moshling into Glumps,' he says.

Great. If that's true, you'll really have a job on your hands.

'Well, I heard he was with Sweet Tooth in the Fun Park, handing out something to the Moshlings.' Mizz Snoots is walking by and must have overheard. With a flick of her hair and a curl of her top lip she looks round at the chaos.

'Does either of you have any idea what on earth's happened to them?' she says as a bunch of Ponies start a completely out of control race up the middle of the street.

'See. Look at them all. I mean, really.' Mizz Snoots clearly isn't impressed.

'They'll carry on like this unless we do something

about it,' you shout, dodging a hoof. 'And poor old Buster's still back at the ranch holding the fort on his own.'

'But what made them turn? They used to be such lovely little things. Well most of them did,' Mizz Snoots says.

'Dr. Strangeglove's made them all go rotten and if I don't find him soon . . .' You let them work out the rest. A city full of permanently naughty Moshlings would be a real nightmare.

You step away unsure of your next step. Do you head for The Port and stop Dr. Strangeglove from unleashing the power of an evil new Glump-a-tron? If so, **turn to page 8.**

Or hope that Mizz Snoots is right and that he's in the Fun Park and you can find a way to stop him? **Turn to page 21.**

You dash into The Puzzle Palace after Bushy. The Musky Huskies are already on the prowl.

'Come here you little scamps,' shouts Bushy as she runs after the lost Fluffies.

'I'll see if I can head them off,' you call out.

'Gotcha,' you yell, flinging yourself in their way but to no avail.

'There's one coming your way now,' calls out Bushy as she herds them forward.

But this is no good at all.

'I can't get hold of them, Bushy. They move too quickly,' you say, trying to grab onto another one.

'Hang on a second, I'll use the net,' she replies, reaching into her backpack.

Suddenly there is a flurry of fur and the Puppies move in. Before too long you have them surrounded.

'One quick flick of the net and then . . .'

Thwack! Down it comes. The Fluffies are completely trapped. Unfortunately so are you.

'Er, Bushy?' you call out as the Moshlings pin you to the ground. You spit out a mouthful of netting.

'Sorry about that. It was a case of all or nothing.' Bushy smiles apologetically.

'Never mind. At least we've got them.'

Now all you have to do is find a way out of the net.

'Ow. Stop that. Leave me be,' you shout wearily, as the Fluffies squash you with snuggles. When will it ever end?

The End

45

In the offices of the *Daily Growl* you find a very busy Roary.

'No time to chat, sorry. With all these badly behaved Moshlings on the rampage there's a fresh story brewing every few minutes. Plus word's just breaking that Strangeglove has invented a new even more powerful Glump-a-tron. I've got to keep my eyes on everything.'

You try to block his way as he rushes about, desperate to get his attention.

'Please Roary. I wouldn't be here if it wasn't important.'

He stops moving for two seconds.

'You're the only one who can possibly help,' you beg. You give him your most desperate and pleading eyes in the hope he'll take pity.

'You've got one minute,' he shouts, leading you into his office. As you go, another big story breaks about some errant Moshlings tearing up the Cotton Clump Plantations.

'Never known anything like it,' says Roary. 'They're totally out of control . . .'

'I'm trying my best to stop them,' you tell him. 'But every time I sort one problem, another comes along that needs solving. Like right now I'm trying to track down some escaped Fluffies that disappeared from Buster's Ranch. I'm scared if I don't find them they'll do even more damage. They've gone off the rails more than any of the other Moshlings put together.'

Roary raises twelve of his eyebrows.

'You've heard something haven't you? Please, if you have, I really need to know where they might be if I'm to find them.'

Roary nods then flicks through a few sheets of paper on his desk.

'Not sure how much good this will do you, but there were a couple of bits of news that filtered through earlier,' he says.

'I'll be grateful for anything that might help. I've tried looking all over the place but found nothing so far,' you say.

Roary continues. 'There were definite sightings of at least two, maybe three, down in the Moshling Garden.'

Your ears prick up at this piece of news. That would make sense with what you saw on your search as well. You were in the Garden earlier looking for them and were convinced you caught a quick glimpse of Flumpy the Pluff rushing by.

Roary waves his paper in the air. 'But that was well over an hour ago.'

'So, there's still a chance they might be there.'

'Of course. Like I say that was the last definite sighting. However . . .'

He glances down at his desk.

'Tyra Fangs was in here not twenty minutes ago and reported seeing something. Sounded to me like it could have been an off the rails Fluffy.'

'Where is she now?' you ask.

'Said she was heading back to the Underground Disco,' he replies, shuffling his papers.

Your mind is reeling. Do you go back to where the escaped Moshlings were last spotted in the Moshling Garden? If so, **turn to page 30.**

Or do you go and see Tyra, who thinks she saw one, even though nobody can be really sure it was a Fluffy? **Turn to page 37.**

You've decided that trying to destroy the evil Glump-a-tron on your own is the only option, so you sprint back to The Port. There it stands, almost mocking you while poor innocent Moshlings are drawn into its clutches, then churned out as smelly looking Glumps. There has to be a way to wipe it out for good. But how?

You walk round it slowly. It's pretty tough looking, with solid metal casing all round. Plus it's really heavy. Still, there has to be a way.

You grab an old tree branch from nearby and try hitting the machine with it but that just seems to make it angry. Moshlings are being dragged in by the dozen. Luckily for you it only seems to be drawing in Moshlings or you too could be hauled inwards.

Hansel, Cutie Pie and Coolio, who happen to be nearby start getting forced towards it against their will. They manage to grab onto your legs, stopping themselves from hurtling into the deep, dark abyss of the machine. You look down and see their pleading eyes. You have to find a way round this, but what if everything you try just makes things worse? You can feel their grips weakening. If you don't do something soon they'll be well and truly glumped.

Suddenly, from the shadows, a figure appears. A figure destined to send shivers up the spine of even the bravest of Moshis. A familiar cackle fills the air.

'Mw-hah-ha-ha-ha-ha.'

It's Strangeglove with his sidekick Sweet Tooth

lurking by his side.

'Did you see how I added the extra "ha-has"' into my evil laugh? I think it makes me sound just that bit more wicked. What d'you think?' he asks.

'We meet again, Strangeglove.' You feel the Moshlings' grip of fear tighten once again on your legs, but know deep down that time is ticking away for these unfortunate fur balls. If you don't stop that machine, their days are numbered.

'You know I will have to destroy your Glump-a-tron,' you say.

'Ha, mwh-ha-ha-ha,' he chortles. 'See what I did there? I tried changing the "ha" and the "mwh" around. Yes I think that definitely makes me sound scarier.'

'Get to the point Strangeglove,' you shout. You cannot stand by and watch even more Moshlings get glumped.

'The point is my Glump-a-trons are built to be indestructible. Throw anything at them and they'll just carry on glumping. And if you hadn't already noticed, I installed a defence mechanism in this one especially. The more you try and attack it, the faster it Glumps; which I thought particularly clever of me. Mw-ha-ha-ha-ha. No I think I like my original evil laugh the most. What do you think Sweet Tooth, 'Mw-ha-ha-ha-ha' or 'Ha-mwh-ha-ha-ha?'

Before you have time to say that you actually think they both work well at making him sound particularly stupid, there is a sudden screeching sound. Strangeglove's low-rider has appeared out of nowhere, seemingly driven by a pile of Glumps. The ones at the bottom must be operating the pedals, while the one at the top is preparing to steer Strangeglove on his path to escape. He laughs evilly one more time, then hops into his getaway car, pulling Sweet Tooth in after him.

'As Strangeglove will have all the Moshlings glumped by then anyway, I may as well tell you; the effects of the sweets only last twenty-four hours. By then it will be far too late for them! ' Sweet Tooth calls out, as the low-rider speeds off.

You turn your attention back to the Glump-a-tron.

Strangeglove really has made it indestructible and the self defence mechanism is definitely working. That thwack across the back you gave it with the branch is making it work at ten times the power. Worryingly, it still feels like it's getting stronger.

Not only are Hansel, Cutie Pie and Coolio heading towards the machine but because they are clutching onto you, you can feel yourself being dragged forwards too. Could this be it? Could the unspeakable happen to you? Never before has any non-Moshling been through the glumping process, but it's rumoured that the effects would be catastrophic. You picture yourself as some sort of part Moshi, part Glump Monster. How would you save the day from Strangeglove's evil master plan if the unthinkable were to happen?

You edge closer and closer towards the Glump-a-tron.

The invisible force is tugging you against your will into the deep, dark depths and an uncertain future. A future that you know cannot end well.

You reach the edge of the Glump-a-tron and grab onto it to try to stop yourself and your three terrified, trouser-clinging Moshlings from hurtling inwards. You feel yourself being pulled closer feet first. This is it. The end of everything you know and the beginnings of glumpdom.

Suddenly a crunching and grinding sound fills the air. The Moshlings bury their heads in fear. A second later the Glump-a-tron grinds to a shuddering halt and you fall back to the floor. You look around. Smoke pours from the machine but otherwise it remains quiet and still. Destroyed. But how? Only then do you notice the cold breeze around one foot. Your shoe must have come off and been sucked in first! You laugh and the Moshlings join in. Strangeglove might have made his machine indestructible to any form of attack but it couldn't cope with your smelly old trainer jamming up its internal workings.

You and the Moshlings lie back, chortling and guffawing. The evil Glump-a-tron is finally destroyed, and now that you know the effect of the sweets won't last forever, the end is finally in sight.

The End

These Moshlings are going cer-azy and the ranch is in a right state. Feathers, Slopcorn, Loopy Liquid everywhere and nothing you try to bring them under control is working.

'We could always try filling them up with Snail Ale. See if that slows them down,' you shout across to Buster, as he launches a pillow counter-attack.

'Nice try but it would never work,' he calls back, dodging a large slice of inbound stale Twistmas pudding.

'It'll make them even sharper and more lethal,' he shouts. 'Snail Ale gives them ideas. They'll just think up even more ways to misbehave.'

You duck for cover and take stock of the situation. Right now it's mostly Birdies inside the Ranch causing all the trouble. But a number of Dinos are heading for the door.

'We've got a breakaway mob forming outside, Buster. What shall we do?'

'You keep this lot covered while I try and head the Dinos off,' Buster shouts as he begins his crawl along the floor; soldier style on elbows and knees. He looks like Burnie the Fiery Frazzledragon on the hunt for gasoline.

You turn your full attention to the Birdies, who are waddling about, swooping overhead and flapping around you. Every one of them was as cute and loveable as can be just a single day ago, but they are now intent on causing as much mischief as possible.

You can sense they are planning on a major attack

from above. DJ Quack is dancing his way across to you with a whoopee cushion under one wing, while Peppy the Stunt Penguin is picking up speed for some sort of sky-based assault.

You are desperately trying to formulate a plan when you hear a noise. Buster has gone. Vanished. Disappeared under a sea of Dinos. His muffled shouting is the only clue to where he currently is.

'Take that. Oh, so, think this is clever do you? Well see how clever you find . . . Ow . . . right, I want the name of whichever Moshling just pulled my whiskers.'

He's having a very hard time of it. He knows his Moshlings well and, usually, exactly how to deal with them. Right now, though, they are being way too naughty. Plus they've all burst past him and are currently outside wreaking havoc in the sunshine.

You have a dilemma. Do you stay here and deal with the Birdies inside the ranch? If so, **turn to page 10.**

Or do you try and help Buster tackle the desperate Dinos outside? In which case, **turn to page 70.**

As you cower behind the Gumball Machine, Jeepers flings another can of Swoonafish at you. This is no good at all. He has things to throw and you don't. Then you spot it. A big box of Mice Krispies by the bookcase. Not nearly as lethal as the cans, but they'll do.

He launches another can but it's his last one. As he heads back into the kitchen to grab some more, you pounce. A quick forward roll out from your hiding place and you have the box. It's full. You somersault back to where you were before and wait.

'Come on, tough guy,' you hiss. Jeepers has no idea you are now armed. He reappears with a can in each paw, his eyes narrowing as he seeks out his prey.

'One, two, three . . .' you count down slowly then spring out, into a crouching position and let him have it. Full in the furry face. Mice Krispies hurled by the dozen. Down he goes, shocked, but only for a second.

'Aaaaaarrggghhh!' you yell, taking a can hit in return. 'Nnnnnnnoooooooooo!!!!' you scream in slow motion. And then again at normal speed when you remember this is real life and you are not on TV.

For a minute or two you let each other have a full attack, square in the chops until you collapse laughing. You are both a bit bruised, but this is just the best game ever. Time to reload because that Moshling is going down. Buster appears by your side, grabbing a handful of Mice Krispies and joins in on a two pronged attack!

The End

You head off in search of the missing Fluffies. You look everywhere but they are nowhere to be seen. Very occasionally amongst the mayhem you might catch a quick glimpse of the floppy ear of Honey the Funny Bunny scuttling past. Or even the odd sight of IGGY the Pixel-Munching Snaffler creeping about in a hedge. After a while of chasing your tail, you sit down. This is no good; no good at all. You need help tracking down those ever-moving little rascals.

Where on earth can they be?

Two thoughts immediately spring to mind. If there's anything going on in Monstro City then Roary Scrawl will know about it. After all, the *Daily Growl* is the news hub. If the Fluffies have been spotted, he should have heard about it by now.

The other option, of course, is to find someone who could actually help you look for them. An expert in the field. Somebody with knowledge. An explorer like Bushy Fandango.

If you think asking Bushy Fandango to help is the best option to try and track down the escaped Fluffies, **turn to page 68.**

If you feel your best bet is to go and see Roary Scrawl and see if he's heard anything, **turn to page 46.**

You dash off to find Babs, doing everything you can to avoid being attacked by the ever-spreading Moshling menace.

Something is thrown. Duck. A Ninja Moshling turns nasty on you. Dodge. You narrowly manage to avoid a pincer movement menace from a pair of Puppies. Weave.

'Babs! Babs! Wait up.' You spot her up ahead, trying to pluck a clump of Chocolate Coated Broccoli out of her hair that an errant Foodie must have hurled at her.

She keeps moving, forcing you to run alongside.

'Oh, no. If you stand still that's when they get you. I've had to shut up shop. The little swines were in there messing with my stock, running off without paying, chucking everything around. What has happened to them?' she asks.

'I really don't have time to explain,' you mutter.

'I smell the evil work of Dr. Strangeglove,' Babs says. 'That or those Moshlings have been letting rip. Pphheew. Either way something is definitely very rotten.'

'Spot on as always, Babs,' you cry. 'And he's got a Glump-a-tron to end all Glump-a-trons, so unless I find a way to reverse the effects or switch it off . . . well let's just say you'd better get used to what happened in your shop becoming a daily occurrence.'

'How can I help?' she asks.

'I can't take it apart unless I can find a diagram of how it was all put together.'

'Say no more. Follow me.' And with that she changes direction and picks up speed.

'I've got all kinds of blueprints and manuals back at the shop. There just might be something in one of them,' she puffs and pants as you run alongside her. 'Anything I can do to stop Monstro City becoming totally overrun with those little beasts.'

Once you reach the shop, completely out of breath but having made good time, Babs disappears into the back. She re-emerges a few moments later with a large dusty box.

'There's a bunch of stuff in here from Strangeglove. Best if you don't ask how we came to acquire it, for your own safety, you understand. Now this might be some sort of a Glump-a-tron design . . . no hang on. Now that I look closely, they're just the instructions for my Bubble Machine. Still every cloud and all that. I've been looking for them for ages.'

You really need Babs back on track here and quickly. Even as you stand there in her shop, Glumps are appearing outside the window at a rapid rate. Only seconds ago they were just regular, if temporarily badly behaved, Moshlings.

'Er, Babs. Could we focus here please? Concentrate on the job at hand. I mean I hate to worry you or anything but . . .' Your eyes flick back to the menacing Glumps pressed against the glass.

She buries her head deep in the box.

'Ah ha!'

'Found something?' you ask.

'Yes. Not the blueprint but I did always wonder what happened to that sandwich.'

You are getting seriously impatient now.

'Wait. Could this be any use?' she cries.

And out comes some rolled up sheets of yellowing paper. Babs blows the dust off one and lays it out flat. It's only a rough sketch but it looks for all the world to you like an early version of Strangeglove's Glump-a-tron. There are one or two others of a similar design as well.

'Probably just a prototype but it'll do. Definitely the best we've got to work with. I mean they all seem to follow roughly the same pattern. Three wires control the circuit, so if I cut this one. No. That might just make things worse. That one seems to lead . . .' You break off confused.

The blueprints are all fairly similar but there are a number of major differences. You will just have to trust your judgement.

'Thanks Babs,' you say, grabbing the blueprint and a pair of scissors and heading for the door.

'Let me know how it all turns out,' Babs calls after you. 'Good luck.'

You rush off with all the strength you can muster, reaching the Glump-a-tron down at The Port. It's still dragging in Moshlings by some evil Strangeglove force. Moshlings cling to anything they can grab onto, but are then forced to let go before being hurtled noisily into the machine's terrible mouth.

You unfold the blueprint and prise the back panel off the Glump-a-tron. Yep. Sure enough. Three wires. You look back at the blueprint. The red wire seems to be linked to the power. The green wire looks like it controls the glumping mechanism and the brown wire would seem to take care of the speed at which glumping occurs. A bead of sweat runs down your face. Get this wrong and everything could end in disaster. Everything relies on you. You nervously look back at the blueprint. Hang on a minute. Have you got this right? The brown wire looks like it might split off and head back on itself towards the main control switch, which means it should be the one to cut. But what if your first instinct is right? If you follow the red wire on the blueprint then it looks like it starts and ends with the power supply.

You have one last glance then take a deep breath. You just have to follow your instincts. You snip the red wire and wait. At first there's a loud rumbling noise from the Glump-a-tron and then . . . silence. You wait nervously. Have you got it all wrong and made everything ten times worse?

No. Your instincts were right! Any interference with the other two would have been a disaster. The Glump-a-tron finally stops glumping and, all around you, relieved Moshlings are starting to smile once again. They look over at you; the hero of the hour!

The End

Your decision to head for the volcano with Bushy Fandango is a good one. As you arrive you discover the missing Fluffies. You do a quick head count.

'All here?' asks Bushy.

'Everyone present and correct,' you confirm.

'Then you no longer need me.'

You shake your head.

'Not quite I'm afraid. You see they still need to be rounded up and knowing the way they keep running off, it's not going to be easy,' you say.

Bushy watches for a second or two.

'They'll be no problem for my Musky Huskies. As the only Moshlings not to have been in contact with the sweets, they are ready for anything.' And she brings her fingers to her lips in order to whistle them into action. You stop her.

'The thing is. Even if we can control them, there's still the matter of Dr. Strangeglove to deal with. I've somehow got to work out how to reverse the effect of those sweets.'

'And you really think he'll just tell you?'

'He might let something slip while he's boasting in front of his Glumps.'

Bushy looks at you in horror.

'You don't mean . . .'

'It's the only way,' you say. 'I'm going to have to disguise myself using a Morph stone and infiltrate his hideout.'

Bushy shakes her head.

'Have you any idea how dangerous that could be? What if you can't turn yourself back? What if . . .'

You hold up a paw. 'Please Bushy. It's something I have to do. Just take care of the Fluffies for me.'

And with that you are gone. Back to deal with Dr. Strangeglove once and for all by glumping yourself. Could this be the worst decision you have ever made?

Turn to page 39 to find out.

You are still very much under attack from IGGY . . .

'Ow!' He's actually trying to bite you. It's not too painful. More of a nip than a full on chomp but it still stings. He then sort of flaps round as if trying to swat at you. Not easy when he has no arms.

'Stop that will you?' He tries another gobble, as you work out what must be going on. He clearly thinks you're a cursor of some sort.

'Well I'm not,' you call. 'Stop trying to eat me!'

But it's no good. He's got you in his sights.

'Right, that's it.' That last nip was the final straw. You have to make yourself invisible somehow. You try rolling up in a ball. If he thinks you look like an arrow he'll keep confusing you with a computer's cursor but it's no good.

'Power surge!' you shout back at him in the hope that it scares him off. It doesn't. He's still after you.

'Delete all,' still no joy. 'Log off!' you shout. But he continues to try and munch you.

'Hang on a second.' You've thought of something. 'This calls for a bit of nifty mouse work.' You say to yourself.

You dart about as fast as possible. And it seems to be working. He tries a couple more munches before giving up and heading back to cyberspace.

You sit down and try to catch your breath. That was never going to be easy but at least you've shaken him off.

But you still need to find the rest of those Fluffies.

Turn to page 16 to continue the hunt.

You've got to find a way to stop the Glump-a-tron from glumping. Even as you are standing there, another three Moshlings have been through it and come out as something very strange looking. One is now a snaggle-toothed brute with enormous eyebrows. Another has three eyes and the most ridiculous curly quiff you have ever seen. The third is sitting in a pool of its own drool. Yuck!

You know you won't be able to disable the machine yourself, so you need to find someone who can. There's Babs of course. She might not be that handy when it comes to using a screwdriver, but she does stock all kinds of rare and exotic items. She may just have some kind of Glump-a-tron instruction manual. Or you could try to get hold of Dewy. He's a real DIY kind of a guy and there is a chance he might be able to disable it somehow.

If you think getting hold of the blueprint from Babs is the way forward, **turn to page 57.**

If you think Dewy is the man to help, you need to track him down by **turning to page 41.**

You arrive in the Market Place and spot them straight away.

Big Bad Bill the Woolly Blue Hoodoo is leaping out from behind the stalls shouting **'Booo!'** Kissy the Baby Ghost is pretending to be really cute so passersby will stop and say 'Aaahhh,' at which point she roars **'Rrrrraaaggghhh!'** in their faces, terrifying the living daylights out of the poor unsuspecting monsters. And Ecto the Fancy Banshee is charging round flapping his shimmering cape, so the mysterious electric wobble-plasma inside turns everything it touches inside out. And then he just collapses with laughter. Wow! Tyra was right. These guys are a handful. As you try to decide on your next move you hear a creepy noise behind you.

'Mw-ha-ha-ha-ha.'

You don't need any further clues. You can tell exactly who it is by the reaction of everyone in the Market Place. You spin round to face him. Dr. Strangeglove and his rotten accomplice, Sweet Tooth, are clutching bags of the sweets that began this nonsense in the first place. You stare at them as they circle you menacingly.

'Did you not hear me? I said Mw-ha-ha-ha-ha,' Strangeglove continues but you refuse to let him see how scared you are.

'I heard you all right.' You step forward to show you mean business. 'I also heard that you smell of cheese but I'm trying not to let the stench bother me.'

This sets the Spookies off and within seconds they

are dashing about, laughing and bumping into each other. Strangeglove tries not to look concerned.

'Mw-ha-ha-ha-ha. You see. My evil laugh shows just how not bothered I am by your pathetic insults. For I am the creator of all this. All the madness before you is the work of my twisted mind. Every badly behaved Moshling and glorious Glump is a result of my handiwork. So telling me I smell of cheese only makes me laugh.'

You realise quickly that all this bravado stems from the fact that there's no way you can take him on alone and he knows it. But the Spookies have heard everything he had to say and a sudden change comes over them. Big Bad Bill has spotted Sweet Tooth's shiny red nose and mistaken the candy-coated criminal for a clown, and Big Bad Bill really hates clowns . . .

'Mw-ha-ha-ha-ha,' Strangeglove chuckles again, just to prove the point. But he isn't chuckling for long.

The Spookies are circling. Strangeglove's smile begins to fade as Ecto moves in, followed by Big Bad Bill and Squidge the Furry Heebee. They prepare themselves to launch with Kissy fluttering gently in the breeze above. All four are ready and waiting to attack.

Suddenly, they pounce! Before Strangeglove can say **'AAAAAgggghhhh!'** which he does pretty soon afterwards, he is buried beneath a monstrous pile of badly behaved Moshlings, along with Sweet Tooth. It's your turn to smile as you watch them sink in a sea of Spookies. A single gloved hand slowly emerges from below, held aloft, before slowly disappearing beneath the pile once again.

You know they won't do any permanent harm to the two wicked ones. They might have turned naughty but they're still Moshlings deep down. There's a little part of you that can't help but think it's a shame. Strangeglove is responsible for all of this wreckage you see before you. However, you know that wanting hurt to be caused to anybody, even someone as vile as him, would make you just as bad. Instead you just enjoy the spectacle of him being well and truly spooked. As Squidge nips away at him, Big Bad Bill prods Sweet Tooth into submission with his mystical Staff of Power. Now it's their turn to wait for the effects of the sweets to wear off. You put your feet up and settle back to watch the show, thinking for the first time today that there really is no rush whatsoever.

The End

You spend ages looking for Bushy Fandango and eventually track her down in the Bizarre Bazaar. She is unpacking treasures and curios from her latest expedition to the Yappalation Mountains.

You burst in shouting, 'Help!!'

'Slow down will you?' she says. 'This little gem's a Spicy Dragon roll. A little cracker with one very special twist . . .'

'Sorry Bushy, but this is really important. Some escaped and out of control Moshlings need tracking down. So I thought "who better to ask than the greatest explorer of them all?" Can you help?'

She pauses for a second.

'If you mean the Fluffies I saw drawing on walls and fighting with each other earlier, then they were heading North. I should be able to track them down for you but you need to decide where to start looking. By my calculations they'll either be up near the Volcano or, looking at the speed they were travelling, maybe somewhere around The Puzzle Palace.'

You look at her, torn. Decisions, decisions, decisions.

Do you head for the Volcano?
If so, **turn to page 61.**

Or hope you can round them up in The Puzzle Palace?
Turn to page 19.

The Moshlings are all still staring at you. Nobody's going to own up as to who kicked that ball.

There's only one thing for it. It's time to embarrass them into giving in. You start dancing and let them see your best moves. They are clearly mortified but admit it.

'No? Then prepare for a torture worse than death. It's time . . . to sing.'

The poor Moshlings can hardly believe their ears.

'Oh yeah. I'm in the grrooooooovvveee, baaaaaybbbbbyyyy!!!' you screech.

They are beside themselves with embarrassment.

'Ready to tell me who kicked that ball yet?' you ask, breaking off from the song for a second.

'Well then. Don't say I didn't warn you . . . Stand back as I sing and dance at the same time. Oh yes.'

And giving it a twirl and a bit of jive boogie you turn the volume up to max.

'Coz I'm a moooooooovvvvvveeerr and a shhhaaaaakkkeeerrr yeah!'

The Moshlings have had enough. They turn and point at Mini Ben. He is horrified at being ratted out so quickly but immediately bing bongs very, very apologetically.

You smile. It was a sure fire plan right from the start.

'Thank you. There. Now that wasn't so hard was it?'

And you wander off to relax. You won't be having any more trouble from those Moshlings now that they know what you are capable of.

The End

You rush across to where Buster is lying. He has taken quite a hit from the Dinos.

'Buster! Are you OK?'

'Do I look it? I've been rummaged by Doris the Rummaging Plotamus. Danced on by Gurgle the Performing Flappasoaurus. Cuddled to within an inch of my life by Snookums the Baby Tumteedum. And well and truly potted by Pooky the Potty Pipsqueak.'

Still he put up a good fight. The battering of naughtiness that he's had to contend with would be enough for anyone. It's a sign of his understanding of Moshlings and sheer strength that he's managed to hold them off for so long.

He leans forward, pulling you down to him.

'I can't go on . . .' he whispers. 'It's up to you now. You have to deal with them alone . . .'

The effort of croaking at you has been too much and he lies back, his whiskers bristling as he breathes deeply. You prop him up against a Rainbow Chair then dash outside into the yard. You are worried about him but he's as tough as Big Boots and, as Buster says, you have a job to do now.

It's chaos out here. The Dino's are running amok and the yard is starting to look like a rubbish dump. You try chasing after a couple of them but it's a losing battle. They are far too quick and there are far too many of them. It's hopeless.

Suddenly the Dinos start whining. It's a noise like fingernails being screeched down a blackboard. It's horrible. You then feel a pawing sensation and look down. You are completely surrounded by Dinos and all of them are whining away and grabbing you for attention. It's as noisy as the first day of the sales on Gift Island!

Over the screeching you can just about work out what a few of them are after. It seems Pooky and Squidge want to play a game, while Doris and Snookums are complaining that they're hungry. You can't actually make sense of the others but they're also demanding attention of some sort.

You sigh deeply. You'd better do something or they will never shut up.

If you decide to feed the hungry ones,
turn to page 23.

If you decide to try your best to organise a game,
turn to page 72.

You gather the Moshlings together for a game as best you can. It's a bit like herding Kitties. Not that you've ever tried herding Kitties before but you can imagine this is exactly what it would feel like.

'Right everyone. What we playing then?' you sigh wearily as you survey the chaos currently erupting around you. All different kinds of Moshlings are causing trouble together. It's even worse than when they stick to their own kind.

'Roxy, stop that!' you shout as she sprinkles vinegar over Cleo.

This is going to be a lot harder than you thought.

'Chop Chop! That's so not funny,' you call, as he chucks a stink bomb at Mr Snoodle.

This is not a game. Well it might be a game if the game were called "run round each other, head butting one another while the other one tries to trip the first one over."

'I'm not warning you again, General Fuzuki!' you say, as he reaches towards Scamp's inflatable frog suit with his pointy sword.

Squidge has now turned his attentions on you and is trying to nip away at you, chuckling evilly.

'Stop that. Ow! Really not funny.' Your patience is wearing thin.

'Ow! Oooh! Aaaagghh.' You try desperately flapping away at Squidge to get him to stop, but nothing seems to be working.

'What about that game we talked about then? Why

don't we try hide-and-seek? You all go off and hide and I'll come look for you.'

Fat chance. Your plan is to get them to hide, then leave them there as long as possible.

'That's it, Lady Goo Goo. Off you go. Try to find somewhere I'll never think of looking.'

First she tries hiding in a box. It's not the best place as it's right in front of you, but at least she's trying. If only the same could be said for Squidge, whose idea of hiding consists of flying in front of your face blowing raspberries.

'Pppplllllpppppp!' Whoa. That Moshling could really use a mint. All those garlicky croutons have made his breath really stinky.

'What are you doing now, Scamp? That's so not hiding.'

You shake your head in frustration. Who knew anything could be so tiring?

To stay here and keep trying to get the Moshlings to play a game, **turn to page 28.**

Or to find a completely new activity for them altogether, **turn to page 76.**

You are outside The Puzzle Palace, doing your best to deal with the bombardment of water balloons currently being hurled at you. Those Fishies are definitely up to no good.

Splat! Yup. That one was thrown by Blurp the Batty Bubblefish. He dives back into the stream he leapt out of, chuckling to himself.

'Eeeerrrr!' you shout. 'That's not water.' As the bomb burst, you immediately realised it was filled with multi-coloured gloop. You look like a rainbow-coloured but slightly smelly cake.

'That's so gross,' you mutter, wiping it from your eyes.

Another bomb hits you square on.

'Right that does it,' you call out, as Cali the Valley Mermaid swims off giggling.

What to do? They have you cornered. Another blast of gloop bursts on your head.

'I know that was you, Stanley,' you call out. Is an all out attack the best option here? You'll never take them on at their own game. This calls for bribery.

'All right Fishies,' you shout. 'Stop that and a round of carpuccinos at Starfishbucks is on me.'

No answer. Another gloopy water bomb flies out of the water and narrowly misses you.

'OK, OK. As much as you can eat at Starfishbucks, followed by tickets to the latest Koi band gig. Plus I'll even throw in a bag of Codcorn.'

You wait for a second. The water bombing seems to have stopped. And the beauty of this plan is that

Fishies are so easily distracted. Once you've got them to Starfishbucks, you won't need to follow up on your side of the deal as they won't remember why they went there in the first place. You really are a genius.

The End

Right, so the game didn't work. Now what? The Moshlings seem even more excitable and rowdy than before. You can see it'll all end in tears. Somebody's bound to get hurt very soon unless this stops. You spot a stray football in the corner.

'Who fancies a kick about?' That should keep a load of boisterous Moshlings occupied for a short while and hopefully help them blow off a bit of steam.

'Two teams. Kitties on this side. Ponies up there. I'll ref.'

Before you can even whistle to say the game's started, they're off, jumping on each other, elbowing and slide tackling . . .

'Oi! Gigi's on your team.'

Fouling each other, grabbing, diving . . .

'Right, Waldo. That's a definite yellow card,' you say. 'All right, Gingersnap. That's a straight red. You're off.'

He can protest as much as he likes but that was a definite lunging tackle on his own teammate. Honestly, the amount of fouling going on here is really quite shocking.

'If this carries on much longer we'll have to abandon the match,' you warn them.

The match is abandoning you, to be more precise. This is sheer and utter chaos. And then . . .

Clunk! The ball smacks you on the head.

You never even saw it coming. To be fair it must have been a great free kick. They're all standing a long way off and would have had to curve it right round to get that kind of an angle on it.

'OK, so who was that?'

Nobody moves. Nobody owns up. You walk round slowly, scanning their eyes for any signs of guilt but they all just shuffle about trying not to look at you.

'Well it must have been somebody,' you say.

Still nothing. You are losing patience.

'All I want is the Moshling that kicked the ball at me to say sorry. Then we can get on with playing nicely.'

Not a sausage.

'It must have been one of you . . . I'm waiting,' you say.

These Moshlings are really pushing their luck. 'If that's the way it's going to be, then we can all just stand out here until one of you owns up.'

Still nothing, but loads of giggling.

'We've got all day,' you say, waiting for one of them to crack.

However, before anyone does so, Buster crawls through into the yard.

'Major problem alert. The Fluffies have escaped from the ranch and they are the worst affected by the sweets. I'm really worried about what they'll get up to,' he says.

To stay put and try and get the Moshling that kicked the ball at you to own up, **turn to page 69.**

To chase after the Fluffies, **turn to page 56.**

ISBN: 978-1409390541

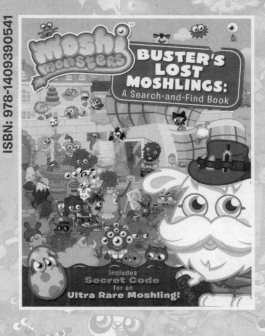

ISBN: 978-1409390527

ISBN: 978-1409390770